Naughty Puppy's First Christmas

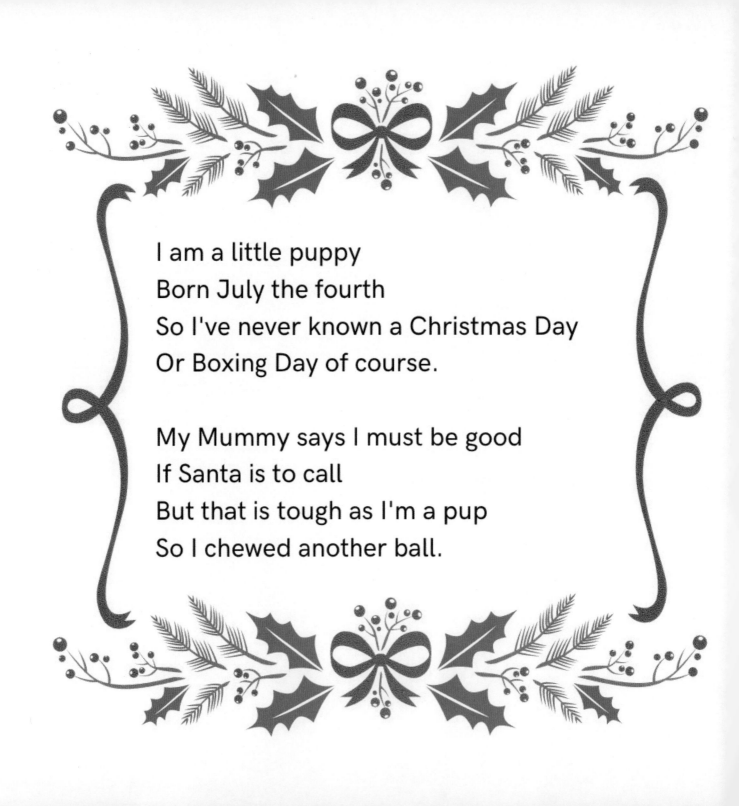

I am a little puppy
Born July the fourth
So I've never known a Christmas Day
Or Boxing Day of course.

My Mummy says I must be good
If Santa is to call
But that is tough as I'm a pup
So I chewed another ball.

I've heard that puppies grow so quick
And play with toys a lot.
I've lots of balls and fluffy things
Oh, what a lot I've got!

Sometimes I am a naughty pup
I'm choosy with my food.
But when I chewed my Mummy's shoes
I knew that I was rude.

The other day, I was so bad
I dug holes in the lawn.
My Mum was very angry
And she wished I'd not been born.

I went out in the garden
To think about my fate.
I was sorry I was naughty
Then I saw the open gate.

If Mummy does not want me
I will run away from home!
So I ran right through the gate
And out along the road.

But I was very frightened
I'd never been alone
The world is very big out there
And I wished I was at home.

I came across a busy road
But couldn't see a gap
To cross the road with confidence
And I didn't have a map.

I tried to cross the busy road
But cars kept moving past
And if that lorry hits me,
My life is over fast!

But a little girl was helpful
And told me to take care
She stopped the cars like magic
So I trotted over there.

But as I left the streets behind
I began to feel quite chilly
It was getting dark and snow came down
And the road was getting hilly.

I felt quite sorry for myself
And looked around for cover
I went inside a farmer's barn
But in there was another!

A big bad dog began to growl
I whimpered in my terror
I backed away towards the door
I'd gone in that barn in error!

I ran and ran away so quick
So pleased I'd got away!
But this is not how things should be
For pups on Christmas Day.

I'd turned around and ran for home
When I met a scruffy mutt.
"Are you lost?" he asked,
"I know a good shortcut."

The scruffy dog was wet and cold
And said he was a stray
HIs humans couldn't keep him
So they turned him out one day.

As we walked, we talked a lot,
And soon were back in town.
"Why run away on a snowy day?
You really are a clown!"

"You clearly have a lovely home
And a Mum who loves her pup.
I wish I had a Mum like that,
I would never give her up."

He asked why I had run away
I told him Mum was cross
She didn't want me any more
I thought I'd be no loss.

I chewed her very favourite shoes
She really was put out
Mum really didn't want me
Of that I had no doubt.

That scruffy dog he laughed at me
"My word! You are so silly,
Mummies sometimes do get cross
But she loves you, Silly Billy!

He said that I should run on home
For Christmas with my folks
"It's not much fun out on the streets,
It's cold and it's no joke."

He said if he could have a wish
There's one thing he'd request
A warm and loving family home
For Christmas, as a guest.

I said, "You're right, I must go home,
I know Mum will forgive me!
But you are coming, too, because
You'll stay for Christmas with me."

"You are coming home and then
I will share my Mother.
It will be a lovely Christmas,
You can be my brother!"

So we set off down the road,
Happy boys together
Even though it snowed on us
We didn't mind the weather.

At last, my house came into view
"We're here!" I said, with glee
But Scruffy was so worried
"What if they don't like me?"

I said, "Who is being silly now?
Come in and say hello!
All my family will be there
Pleased to meet you, I know!"

My Mum cried when she saw us
So happy I was home
And she loved our little Scruffy
And said, "No more you roam!"

"But one thing has to happen
Before we take you in -
It's the bath for you, my lad!
You smell so awfully grim."

Although he didn't like the bath,
Our Scruffy dog was glad
That I had run away that day
Because I was so bad.

We might have never met at all
And he would still be sad
But now he has a family
And everyone is glad.

And so my first big Christmas
Was a very jolly day
With lots of toys and presents
From Santa Claus's sleigh.

And I also gained a brother
A Christmas wish came true
I will gladly share my mother
And all my family, too!

If I could have another wish
I'd wish for a good home
For all the stray dogs in the world
Who are starving and alone.

My new brother fits in well
I love him oh so much!
He'll never be so sad again
With Mummy's tender touch.

MERRY CHRISTMAS

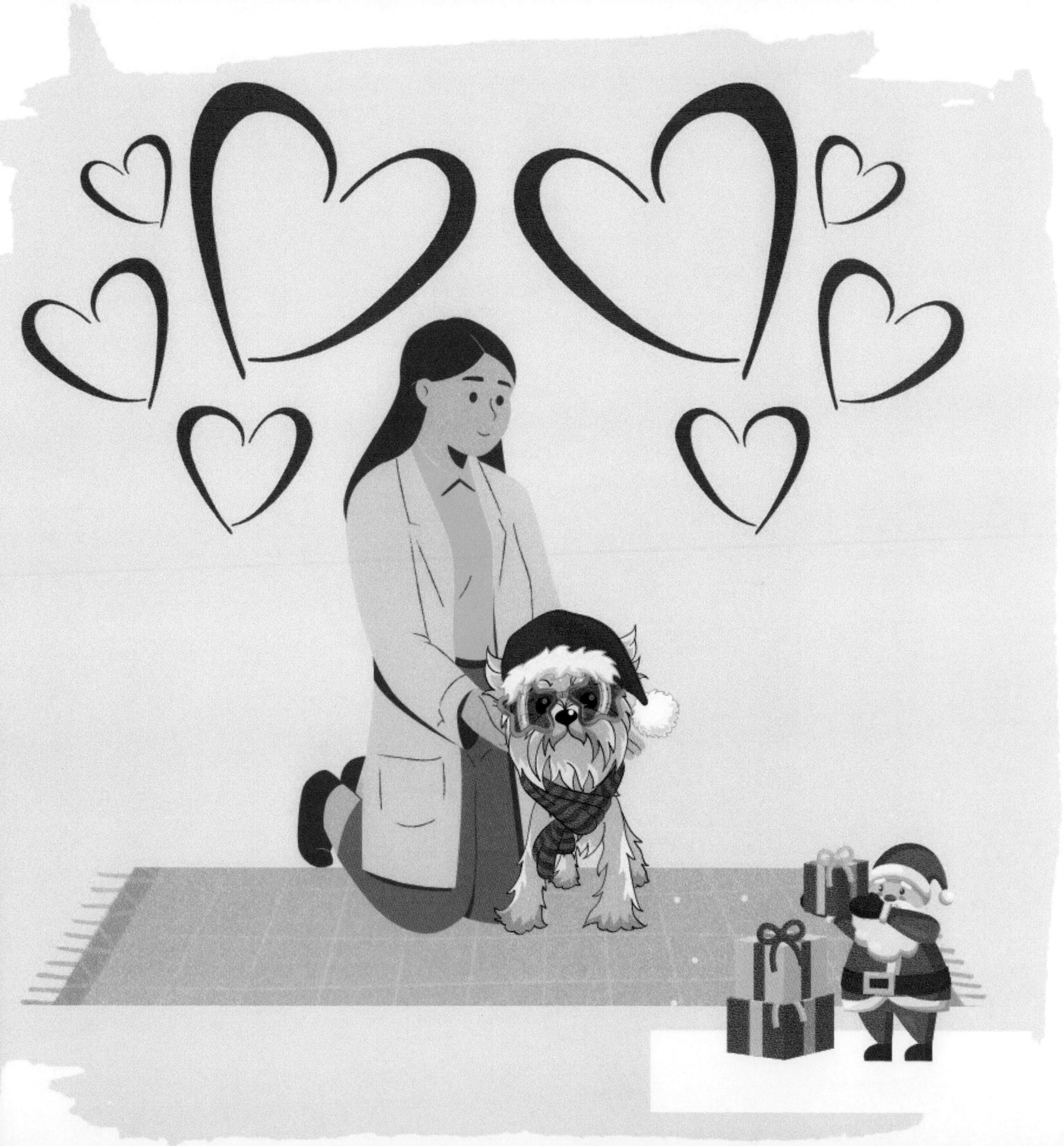

Printed in Great Britain
by Amazon

13034778R00022